Submissive Training

Thrilling And Uncensored Guide To Be A Naughty Dominant

By: More Sex More Fun Book Club

Hey,

Thank you very much for choosing this book!

Before we begin...

If you are interested in non-fiction sex books, head over to our partner site alexandramorris.com

Alexandramorris.com is a great site in the making. They publish e-books, paperbacks, audiobooks and blog posts written by up-and-coming writers and great freelancers. They also give away TONS of Audible coupon codes, Amazon gift cards, pdf copies of books totally free!

We really hope this books will give you valuable information to take your sex life to the next level. Enjoy and please leave an honest review after finishing it.

Best regards

Table of Contents

Introduction

Chapter 1: BDSM and the Community

Chapter 2: Role Play – The Submissive-Dominant Relationship

Chapter 3: Tools and Toys for the Dominant Role

Chapter 4: Safety and Techniques

Chapter 5: Outside the Dungeon: Getting Started

Chapter 6: More BDSM Techniques for the Bolder Dom

Chapter 7: Qualities of a Dominant

Chapter 8: Rules for a Dom

Chapter 9: Signs of Someone Who is a Non-Dominant

Conclusion

BONUS: Preview of our fiction book Taming the Tigress: A Journey To Submission

    Chapter 1: Caged

    Chapter 2: The Tigress

Introduction

I want to thank you and congratulate you for downloading the book, ***"BDSM Playbook: The Secret Guide to Being the Dominant."***

Thanks to 50 Shades of Grey, BDSM has gotten more attention than ever. Unfortunately, the novel doesn't really provide neither a comprehensive nor accurate look into the lifestyle.

If you are curious in finding out how BDSM works, and would like to be part of the community as a Dom personality, this book is for you! By the end of this book, you should have the firsthand knowledge and confidence to foray into the life of BDSM kink, and associate yourself with people who can teach you more!

Thanks again for downloading this book. I hope you enjoy it!

Chapter 1: BDSM and the Community

BDSM stands for Bondage, Dominance, Submissive, and Masochism. It has gotten quite a reputation after the popularity of 50 Shades of Grey which gives a glimpse into the world of BDSM. However, the book and the movies don't really give an accurate presentation of how this lifestyle works. In this eBook, we'll offer you a rare look into how BDSM works, specifically on the side of the Dominant Role. Note that it's not all about lashings and being the "Boss" in the relationship. You'll find that as a Dom, you'll have to consider other factors in order to be accepted into the community.

Are You Sure You're Into BDSM?

Not just because you think it's hot to tie your partner up during sex does NOT mean you're into BDSM and take the role of a Dom. Try to make a list of what BDSM features you'd like to try out and introduce them to your partner. It's perfectly acceptable if you don't know exactly how BDSM will affect your overall sexual experience since for the most part, people have no idea how the lifestyle works. Generally speaking, BDSM does NOT have sex as its end result. The sex is simply incidental with the pain and discomfort being the primary goals.

If your goal, however, is sex but with a bit more action, then you're not really into BDSM. Chances are you still want sex, but what to make things more exciting. A little leather, a little bondage, and a little exercise in power are not a problem in sex, but it doesn't automatically translate to BDSM. That doesn't mean you shouldn't experiment, however, since you'll never really know unless you try.

Who Is a Dominant?

The Dominant is the one who takes control of the situation. More aptly put, this is the individual who decides what will happen inside the room. Traditionally, the dominant is the one who holds the whip, restraints, or inflicts pain on the submissive. Anything the Dom wants done is followed by the Sub under the cloak of no limitations. Of course, there are actually limitations, but having no limits as to what you can do is part of the fantasy. Typically, the Dom and Sub must talk about the situation before plunging into it beforehand.

Who Is a Submissive?

The Submissive or the Sub is the one who follows orders. They are the ones who are restrained, whipped, or who do whatever is requested by the Dom in the interest of role play. You'll understand later on that one of the hardest parts about BDSM is finding the perfect Sub who fits your personal preferences. For now however, it's important to first define the important qualities and roles of the Dom which will be discussed later.

BDSM Services

The BDSM community is popular enough that there are currently facilities catering to BDSM requirements. You have probably heard of facilities composed of several rooms where BDSM activities are held. These are special types of facilities that often offer an array of professional Submissive-types who will do your bidding.

Now the question is: how do you find these facilities in your community? We'll talk about that later in the Chapter. Of course, it's usually better if you find a sexual partner who is also happy to play the role of the Submissive.

The Community

The Community is fairly tight knit and despite the popularity of 50 Shades of Grey, the fact is that the BDSM lifestyle is still under much scrutiny. This is why it isn't surprising that the BDSM community stays low and is rarely advertised so blatantly. The internet is one of the best places to learn about the lifestyle but as for the real-world, you will need to be in contact with people in order to be part of it in the truest sense. BDSM functions much like a secret society wherein you have to meet the right people and prove your interest before being handed a passport or a map towards the center of the community.

One thing you should keep in mind is that being a closely held community, those who favor BDSM have made unofficial rules in the conduct of the Dom and the Sub for the control and protection of both. Many of these will be tackled later but for the most part, understand that there are certain regulations set forth under this lifestyle. The rules may vary from one BDSM facility to another, so it's up to you to learn what they allow and forbid.

Wait, So Is This Legal?

The short and simple answer is – YES. However, the intricacies of it can be quite complicated. Generally speaking, prostitution is illegal in the United States and prostitution is defined as the performance of a sexual act in exchange for money.

BDSM however, is not always about sex. In fact, within the regulated community, there is no sex involved and thus, no law violated. In fact, BDSM facilities go through the routine checks performed by the authorities to ensure that the building is up to code when it comes to fire hazards, earthquake, electrical wirings, and the like.

However, there are instances when BDSM has an element of sex added into it. If you are part of a BDSM Club made up of private people, then it's likely that the BDSM/Sex interplay is purely consensual with no exchange of money between the parties. If you and your partner also enjoy BDSM play within a committed relationship, then this should not be a problem.

Safety During Role Play

The first concern in BDSM is safety. Although inflicting pain and discomfort is inherent in bondage, the intention is to be able to do this without causing excessive injury to a person. Bearing in mind the different tools utilized in BDSM, it's not uncommon for Subs to go home with the beginning of a bruise on their skin – but as much as possible, the community wants to limit telltale effects to bruises on the skin. Blood and broken bones are best avoided and in all cases; instances of this will prompt the Sub to speak out the safe word.

Later on, this eBook will discuss how to perform the different facets of a BDSM Dom without going beyond the lines.

Learning the Language

BDSM is just not a community – it's a lifestyle, which accounts for the fact that they have their own language. Here's what you should know before diving into the community:

Adult toy chest/ toy bag

This is a person's collection of "toys". Usually it's the Dom who has this covered.

Alligator clamp

This is a kind of a nipple clamp that looks like an alligator jaw. Most alligator clamps have adjustable screws with rubber tips.

Animal Transformation Fantasy

This is when the sub assumes the role of different specie which can be a dog, a horse, or a cat. It can also be enhanced by *Animal Play* wherein the sub not only acts but also dresses up as the animal they're supposed to be.

Aftercare

This is an important part of every Dom-sub interaction after the play session wherein the two snap out of their roles and talk about the events that transpired and what they feel about it. This is important to help both the Dom and the sub to get back to normal levels.

Ageplay

This refers to daddy/daughter or mommy/baby situations. The focus here is not on incest but rather, on the nurturing aspect of the relationship. In some cases however, ageplay may also refer to relationships where there is a marked gap between the two participants. For example, a teacher-student role play is quite common for many.

Auction

Adding a bit of spice into the whole experience, an auction essentially involves the sub with Doms bidding for an individual they want to be their slave. Note that this is usually on a temporary basis.

Anal Torture

The act of inflicting pain on the anus.

Bad Pain

Bad pain is essentially the kind of pain that is not mutual or not consensual during the play. It must be kept in mind that BDSM involves pain – but such is consensual pain or within the bounds accepted by the sub or carry a purpose to the play. Anything beyond that is considered Bad Pain and should be avoided.

Ball gag

You insert this rubber ball into the submissive's mouth and hold it in place with a strap.

Ball torture

This may cause pain to a man's testicles, but you can adjust the pain level until the submissive gives in.

B &D, B/D, B/d

This stands for bondage and dominance.

BDSM

This is the acronym for **B**ondage and **D**iscipline, **D**ominance and **S**ubmission, **S**adism and **M**asochism.

Black Sheet Party

An orgy for people practicing BDSM.

Body art or modification

You alter a part of the body, for example, by drawing tattoos or branding a person. You could also pierce the skin, stretch, or inflict scars.

Bondage

Involves physical restraint of the sub, typically involving handcuffs or a tie and in some instances, it may be limited to just a certain body part, such as in Breast Bondage. This also refers to making the person helpless and partially immobilized. You do this by tying the arms and legs of your partner and making him/her submit to all the things you desire in bed.

Bottom

The sub (as opposed to the Top or the Dom).

Breath Control

Play wherein the Dominant takes control of the breathing of the sub.

Boot licking

You ask your partner to lick your (the Dom) boots as a sign of submission.

Branding

This is a permanent scar that Dominant puts on the skin of the submissive. You can do this by applying heated metal to the skin of your lover.

Brat

When a submissive tries to gain the Dom's attention by behaving like a spoiled child, he/she is called a brat.

Breast bondage

Men tie up or restrain the boobs. There are many sorts of contraptions for breast bondage.

Bullwhip

This is a long leather whip. It is also heavy.

Butt plug

You may use this for anal play, either for punishment or for entertainment. Either way, you place this toy in the anus of the submissive.

Cage

The submissive lover is in a cage, the smaller the better so that the submissive would not be able to move freely.

Charity

A form of orgasm denial. A person is prevented from achieving orgasm through the use of tools that stop the person from accessing their genitals. For women, this usually involves a chastity belt while for men, a cock cage.

Collared and Collaring

A collared sub is someone who is owned by a Dom in an intimate and loving relationship. Note though that this doesn't mean exclusive since the Dom can have several collared subs. Being collared puts the sub into a *pup* status as opposed to someone who is a *stray*. Collaring is the formal acceptance of a Dom, Master, or Trainer with respect to a sub.

Contract

It outlines the agreement between the Dominant and the submissive regarding their roles in the relationship. This isn't legally binding but sets the rules as to how each one is supposed to proceed in the relationship.

Caning

You use a cane, which is usually made of rattan, on a sub. Warning though: This could be extremely painful on the other person. This is worse than flogging.

Cat o' Nine Tails

This is a fancy term for a whip with nine tails. For added sensation, choose the one with beads or anything knotted on the whip.

CBT/ Cock and ball torture

This is the pain inflicted on the submissive's penis and/or testicles.

Chocolate

Any sexual activity that isn't vanilla is called 'chocolate'.

Clover nipple clamps

These are rubber-tipped or rubber-colored clamps that are connected by a chain. When you pull the chain, the clamps tighten and produce a wild sensation on the sub's nipples.

Coca-Cola submissive

This person obeys the rules of BDSM only when he or she feels she wants to obey them. Also acts like a brat.

Cock ring

You slip this ring around the base of the guy's penis so he could prolong his erection.

Collar

This is worn by the submissive to indicate that he/she belongs to the Dominant. It also means that the sub is the slave of the Top.

Corset

Popular in the old days, the corset gives the woman an hourglass figure. It also accentuates her breasts.

Crop

This is a type of whip used in horseback riding. It leaves a sting on the submissive.

Cupping

This increases the blood flow on a body part and adds sensation to the sub. To do this, place suction cups on the skin. You could also use your mouth to suck in the skin and 'brand' your slave.

D/s:

Dominance and submission.

Dom

Dominant or the one in charge. The one who holds the power in the sexual activity. He/She is the one who controls the play and tortures the submissive.

Dominatrix

The female version of a male dominant. Also called domme.

DM or Dungeon Monitor

This is the person who supervises the play in the dungeon to make sure that both parties stay within limits.

Dungeon

Room or area where the BDSM play happens. This is where the toys and equipment for BDSM are put up.

Edgeplay

These are forms of BDSM play that are on the edge or have the probability of causing harm, either physically or emotionally. It can be quite subjective since D/s has very varying perceptions of what is dangerous and what isn't. Often however, this includes fireplay, gunplay, bloodplay, and breathplay.

Erotic Spanking

Spanking the other party to stimulate sexual arousal.

Extreme restraints

This refers to a bondage device for extreme restraints and should not be used by beginners to BDSM.

Femdom

A female Dominant. This is another name for domme.

Fetish, fetishism

One's fetish is outside the "normal" things that you do in bed. This fetish gives you sexual gratification. For example, some dominants find a fetish in seeing blood in their submissive, so they cut a part of the skin.

Fisting

The Dom (male or female) inserts entire hand into the sub's anus or vagina.

Flagellation

You can stimulate your partner's genitals by whipping or flogging him/her.

Flogger

Often made of leather, the flogger delivers sting.

Freeplay

This is BDSM play but without a power exchange.

Good Pain

As opposed to Bad Pain, this is the kind of pain that is consented to by the other party and usually carries with it a purpose.

Golden Showers

Urination fetish whereby a person enjoys being urinated on or urinating onto another

Hard Limits

BDSM type of play that someone will absolutely NOT do

Hobble skirt

The hobble skirt gives the wearer less room for movement.

Kitten

Usually the term of endearment given to a submissive, also a role ascribed to the sub during animal fantasy.

Lash

This is a blow from an object with a flat surface, usually, like the whip, crop, or paddle.

Leather

Used for whipping and bondage. It is the common fetish in sex and BDSM because it is a very sexy material. It doesn't break too in extreme play.

Leg cuffs

These restrain the sub's ankles.

Limit (hard limits, soft limits)

This is the sub's final boundary. When he/she gives a soft limit, it means that something might change over time. If there is a hard limit, the sub will never permit a certain act.

M/s

This title stands for Master/ slave.

Master or Mistress

This is typically the word used by the sub when referring to the Dom during a scene. Hence, although the Dom is often referred to as "he" in this book, there are also female Doms.

Martinet

This refers to a small or French flogger.

Masochist

This is a person who finds pleasure in pain; the opposite of the sadist.

Munch

A BDSM meeting in a vanilla location or a location that is public and accessible to the public. This is often a social call with each other about past or future BDSM plays.

Nipple clamps

These are sex toys that you attach to the nipples, so they could stimulate the breasts of the wearer. The sub could experience both pleasure and pain.

Nipple torture

This means to make the sub's nipples painful.

Nipple weights

You add or suspend weights from nipple clamps for increased pleasure or pain on the sub.

OTK

This means over the knee, said when you want to spank a partner.

Paddle

This is a wooden or leather flat instrument that you use for spanking your sub.

Pet

This is another term of endearment for your sub.

Pony play

Common in animal fantasies, the sub takes the role of a pony (Which the Dom can ride, tether, or spank).

Power exchange

This is done when the sub willingly hands over control to the Dom for the play or for the rest of the relationship.

Prince Albert

This is a male piercing between the urethra and the penis.

Puppy play

The sub takes the role of a puppy.

Pussy torture

One causes pain to a female's vagina or clit.

ProDom or ProDomme

Professional Dominants charging money for their services.

PlayParty

A BDSM Party.

RPG/ Role play games

You take on various roles like doctor/nurse, teacher/student, and parent/child.

Red

Say this to stop all play.

Restraint

You limit the freedom and movement of your sub.

Ring gag

This is a ring attached to a strap to keep the sub's mouth open.

Rope

This is a usual type of equipment for bondage.

Rubber

This is another fetish material popular in BDSM, like leather.

S&M, S/M

These initials stand for sadism and masochism.

Sadist

A person who enjoys inflicting pain on their partners. They like to see their partners getting tortured because it gives them sexual gratification.

Sadomasochism

This is when a person who feels sexual gratification from sadism and masochism.

Safe, sane and consensual

This is the "slogan" or number one rule in BDSM.

Safeword

The word used by the sub if she wants to stop the scene. Red is the common safe word (like red light). Yellow, on the other hand, means the sub is about to say Red. If the Dom ignores the safe word, he/she is considered unsafe.

Saint Andrew's Cross

It is shaped like a cross and is used in BDSM. The sub is restrained against the Saint Andrew's Cross when the Dom uses this.

Scene

It is a session, a sexual activity between the Dom and the sub, which can be performed in private or in front of other people. It is also the time period for the BDSM play.

Slapper

This paddle produces a loud noise when it hits the skin.

Slave

This is another word for the sub.

Slave contract

When the Dom and the sub have a slave contract, it ensures that whatever act happens between them is consensual and legally unenforceable.

Switcher

This is the kind of person who can take both the Dom and sub role, depending on the scene.

Spanking bench

The spanking bench looks like a picnic table, but is used to restrain or limit the movement of the sub.

Spencer paddle

This is a paddle with holes to give more pain to the sub.

Spreader bar

This bar holds apart the body parts of a sub.

Stocks

The sub's hand and head go through holes while he/she is standing.

Strap-on

A dildo is attached to this belt.

sub/ subby/ subbie/ submissive

This is the person who gives in to the Dom during the power exchange. Also called a slave.

Subspace

This means the sub consents or allows himself to enter or act in a scene.

Suspension

You suspend the sub using harnesses, belts, ropes and chains. Beginners should not use this.

TPE/ Total power exchange

Total Power Exchange or a 24/7 relationship.

Top

The Dominant in a relationship or in a scene.

Topspace

The Dom's state of mind that he/she may participate in a scene.

Topping from the bottom

The sub tries to control the actions of the Dom.

Tweezer nipple clamps

Nipple clamps that look like tweezers.

Vanilla

Someone who is not into BDSM play, also sex that happens outside the BDSM, opposite of chocolate.

Violet wand

According to BDSM practitioners, the violet wand smells of "ozone". Actually, this is a device that sends electrical charges at contact so it could provide stimulation.

Wartenberg wheel

This is also a device that is used to apply sensation. It looks like a pizza cutter, only spiked.

Wax play

The Dom pours hot wax onto the sub's skin during play.

Whipping post

During play, the sub is tied to the whipping post.

Chapter 2: Role Play – The Submissive-Dominant Relationship

Later on, this eBook will discuss how to perform the different facets of a BDSM Dom without going beyond the lines. First however, it's important to talk about the Dom/sub Relationship.

Dom/sub Relationship

If you'll notice, the word Dom is always written with the first letter capitalized while the sub makes use of the small letter. This is in accordance with their roles wherein the Dom takes the Top spot and the sub is also the bottom.

Note that although the Dom is the one in charge, it is the sub that has the power to stop the scene. The Dom therefore needs excellent self-control that will allow him to stop when the sub asks for a reprieve.

Dom and Control

The Dom is the one in charge, but that doesn't make his job easy. In fact, the Dom has to have extreme control over his person and make sure that he doesn't go beyond the Hard Limits and the limits set by safety. He should always keep the welfare of the sub as his first concern while satisfying his personal pleasure. Remember that with BDSM, both the Dom and the sub get off on their particular roles; the trick is to find that balance wherein both of you get your pleasure without going beyond what is allowed.

Pre-Play

What you do before playing is every bit as important as what you do after. Typically however, a pre-play is done for paid-facilities wherein subs will want to find out the extent of your knowledge on BDSM, the kind of scene you want to play, the Hard Limits, and the Soft Limits they have for their person. Pre-Play is also where the Safeword is determined or any other symbol used for the safety of the sub.

Aftercare

Aftercare is often defined as the healing process after the BDSM scene. In fact, most people say that aftercare is part of the play scene and essentially helps the Dom and sub to go back to neutral level. This is because after the end of a scene, the Dom and sub are likely still buzzing over what happened. The Dom is still clinging to his Dominant personality while the sub is trying to recover from the emotional and physical hurdle she was exposed to. By going through aftercare, the Dom and sub manage to adjust their moods and emotional status and resume their original roles outside the dungeon.

Aftercare is incredibly important and is one of the factors that separate an excellent Dom from a bad one. More on how to practice Aftercare will be talked about later.

Safe, Sane, and Consensual

This is essentially the BDSM Mantra or the Golden Rule. It comes in many forms but the essence falls down into these three categories: Safe, Sane, and Consensual.

Safe in the sense that there should be safeguards put in place starting with the safeword, the use of BDSM-approved restraints, and even the presence of a monitor if need be. Sane relates to the purpose of the play. The pain or discomfort inflicted should be in relation to the scene or has a definite purpose. Inflicting pain without any viable reason attributable to the BDSM scene is a Bad Pain and should not be tolerated. Lastly, there's Consensual which means that the sub MUST CONSENT to the play or to the techniques being used in the play.

Chapter 3: Tools and Toys for the Dominant Role

BDSM leads to better sex

Great sex is when you can be free to be yourself with your lover -- no hang-ups, no pretenses. This is what you get with BDSM sex. Imagine how liberating it is to know that you're having sex with the *real* version of your partner.

Great sex requires variety and couples who practice BDSM are constantly expending time and effort in finding ways to make sex more exciting for each other. Trying one sexual adventure after the other enhances your curiosity and your confidence in bed.

Great sex is a result of great foreplay. Often in BDSM sex, there is constant touching involved. It's not the mindless, mechanical coupling that usually occurs during vanilla sex. In order for BDSM sex to work, it requires you to be aware, to be in the present, to be an active participant. And isn't that what a healthy relationship is all about?

BDSM leads to better communication in relationships

In order to have great sex, it's important that you don't just *do* it. You also need to be able to *talk* about it. Keeping all of your needs and fantasies to yourselves inevitably leads to dissatisfaction, frustration, and resentment towards each other. Couples who engage in BDSM are more communicative when it comes to expressing their sexual desires. In turn, they also become more open in expressing their deepest emotions.

In vanilla relationships, couples don't usually talk openly about sex. They don't confront their partner's shortcomings or wonder about their own until such a time when their relationship or marriage becomes threatened. BDSM couples, on the other hand, are naturally honest and direct with each other because they need transparency in order for the BDSM relationship to thrive. In fact, most BDSM couples tend to develop a secret language that only the two of them can understand. Each time you talk about rules and safe words or make a list of things that you want to do between the sheets, you are actively communicating and considering each other's needs.

BDSM increases intimacy between couples

When couples do something new together, this makes them vulnerable to each other. When you share an adventure with each other, the experience binds you. How can it not? You share a secret together. You've shared one euphoric moment after the next. Moreover, that feeling of bliss that you experience each time you try something new is automatically linked to your partner. Thus, when you think of each other, you end up feeling the exciting sensation all over.

This goes without saying but each time you let your lover bind you, or blindfold you, or flog you, it necessitates a high degree of trust which is essential in all relationships.

BDSM promotes fidelity

Contrary to what most people may believe, BDSM relationships do not often lead to lewd sexual behavior, multiple sexual partners, and infidelity. In fact, couples who take BDSM seriously end up investing a great deal of time, energy, trust, and emotion into the relationship that it would be less likely for them to do anything to sabotage their efforts. They are unlikely to risk all the trust and safety that they have painstakingly built. Furthermore, two of the major causes of infidelity are sexual incompatibility and stagnation. Both rarely apply in BDSM relationships.

BDSM aids in improving mental health

Studies reveal that BDSM friendly individuals are less fearful, more open-minded, more secure in relationships, and better at coping with rejection. According to research, BDSM has therapeutic effects to individuals who have experienced psychological trauma in the past. That's because it allows you to express your sexuality without fear or shame. BDSM sex requires you and your partner to be fully present: mind, body, and soul during the interaction and thus the therapeutic powers of BDSM can be likened to that of yoga or mindful meditation.

BDSM lessens psychological stress and anxiety

A scientific experiment revealed that while participating in BDSM activities, the subjects' stress levels have noticeably decreased. Both dominants and submissives reflected lower cortisol levels in their systems. That's because in BDSM sex, you let go of expectations and judgment to give way to physical intensity. While observing both sub and Dom subjects engage in giving and taking pain, scientists discovered decreased blood flow in the prefrontal and limbic pain regions in the brain. This yields a tranquilizing effect, thus lessening anxiety.

BDSM encourages self-advocacy

Who you are in bed is a reflection of who you are in real life. If you're frightened, anxious, or uptight between the sheets, that's who you are at home and at work. Whether or not it is manifested externally, it's who you are inside.

Participating in BDSM sex helps you become more honest and more upfront about your sexual needs. When you learn to confidently speak out in the bedroom by giving a command, that's when you stop being a person who just sits and wait for others to anticipate your needs. When you learn to speak a safe word during BDSM sex, that's when you stop becoming that person who's too afraid to interrupt someone mid-speech regardless of how uncomfortable you're feeling.

BDSM teaches responsibility

Whether you are a sub or a Dom, BDSM teaches you that you are responsible for the quality of your sexual experience. Being a dominant is not about taking advantage of your power to suit only your selfish desires just as being a submissive is not about shutting your brain off so you could let your partner do all the work. BDSM is all about establishing a give-and-take relationship.

Some people mistake the role of the submissive as a powerless position and thus, one that is free from any responsibility. On the contrary, there is a special kind of power that the submissive possesses over the dominant. It's the sub who decides how long he/she will continue to give away his/her control. The moment the sub uses the safe word, the Dom must stop. Once the submissive decides that he/she will no longer relinquish power, the Sub-Dom relationship is over.

Chapter 4: Safety and Techniques

Safety is the most important concern when it comes to BDSM play. As the Dom, you'll be the one to predict the scene and hold the control on how the play proceeds. The main protection of the sub would be the Safeword which may be uttered at any time to stop the play. This is usually done when Hard Limits are tackled. In the previous Chapter, we talked about the Dom-sub relationship and how to foster trust between the two. In this Chapter, we'll try to talk more about how to ensure safety during play.

Note that ensuring safety isn't all lodged onto the Dom. A good sub will be able to arrange herself in such a way that it minimizes any pain, injury or discomfort. As the Dom however, much is in your hands:

Safeword

The safeword can be anything and everything under the sun as long as it doesn't usually come up during the play session. For example 'no' and 'stop' are quite common in BDSM scenes, especially for those who have a fetish for begging and pleading play. The use of out-of-context words therefore become necessary to fully indicate that play time is over. For example, 'pineapple juice' and 'spongebob' are good safeword choices because they're unlikely to come up during the play.

Note though that safewords aren't always possible. What if you're engage in gag play and the sub can't talk? This is where specific actions or symbols come in. The sub may shake her head three times, nod her head three times, raise up three fingers, or push a button somewhere in the dungeon. The signal can be anything as long as the sub has easy access to it throughout the play.

Check In

A 'check in' is a technique to make sure that the sub still gives consent during the play. This is especially true if you happen to be in the middle of a flogging or perhaps starting a natural development to the play. You want to 'check in' with the sub to make sure that you're not going beyond what she allows. A check-in can be something as simple as asking the sub if she still remembers her safeword. This gives the implication that although she knows exactly what the safeword is, she has no desire to use it during the play. Of course, a 'check in' must be thoroughly explained with your sub before the play starts so that she doesn't accidentally blurt out the safeword when you ask.

Set Limits

After setting up a safeword for your sub to use, the next is to set up Soft and Hard Limits to be followed. Soft Limits are those that are subject to change. Perhaps the sub is curious about this type of play and will welcome it when she learns more about the procedure. Hard Limits however are absolutely no-go and will rarely be subjected to change. As a Dom, you should keep this in mind throughout the play.

Flogging, Spanking, and Planking

When it comes to floggers, cheap is definitely worse. The best flogs are those made from deerskin – they can be expensive, but they guarantee the least amount of damage. Cheap flogs can draw blood even when used with less force. Also note that there are danger areas when flogging. The upper back, thighs, and ass are usually the best places because they can be fleshy and are nowhere near vital organs. What you want to avoid is the face, the neck, the region near the kidneys, the stomach, knees, and elbows. These are generally Bad Pain areas in the community. Spanking and planking make use of the same rules and regulations as to where you should hit.

Using Gags

Gags are also a common element of BDSM play, but you have to be very careful when using them on your sub. Generally, a gag should NEVER encompass the nose because this makes it doubly hard for the sub to breathe. Make sure to use a gag that's soft on the skin to avoid abrasions.

Slapping

When hitting the facial area, slaps should be confined to the cheeks and nowhere else. Hitting the eyes, nose, and mouth can be dangerous for the sub.

Restraints

The first rule in restraints is that you should NEVER leave a restrained sub alone in the dungeon, even for a second! A restrained sub is incapable of movement and is exposed to numerous dangers without a Dom there to ensure that nothing bad happens. Remember that this is your play and even though you have a Dungeon Monitor, the Dom/sub is a very unique relationship so that you will be the one who has to remove the restraints. Note that restraints don't just mean ropes – they're also about handcuffs, silk scarves, or any kind of tying implement. It's best to purchase materials specially made for BDSM purposes to prevent abrasions on the skin of the sub.

Ideally, the restraints should be loose enough that they still allow blood flow through the body. A sub should always be on the lookout for tingly or numbing feelings along the limbs that are restrained. It is the role of the Dom to check in once in a while and make sure that there is no blood restriction occurring due to the bondage.

Collaring

Included in the area of restraints is the use of collars which isn't always advertised in BDSM. The truth is that collars can inhibit breathing which can lead to death. As much as possible, collars are discouraged in BDSM – however, if this is really your thing, then we strongly suggest the 'two finger' rule. This means that the collar has to be loose enough that you can insert two fingers in between the skin and collar without any problem. Anything tighter than that is dangerous.

Aftercare

During aftercare, the Dom manages to become more caring as a natural way of deviating from the Dominant mental status he goes into during the scene. The sub, on the other hand, experiences an emotional uplifting afterwards to help level the physical and mental pressure they went through. Here are some examples of how aftercare works:

- Taking a bath or shower together with the Dom administering to the sub in different ways like massaging shampoo or soap.

- Taking care of any cuts and bruises that the sub got through application of creams, band-aids, ice packs, and gels.

- Massaging any of the sore muscles.

- Food and water to rehydrate the body.

- Talking about what happened and allowing the sub to talk about the scene, in some cases involving cries, anger, or any method of self-expression.

- In some cases, the talk can be about what you liked during the scene and what you didn't like

- Cuddling with each other.

- Having sex at a gentler and more leisurely pace with your partner

- Talking about your feelings with each other and how much you love her

- Brushing her hair or applying lotion all over her body

Of course, those are just examples of aftercare. As a Dom, you should be mindful of the kind of aftercare your sub needs. The more stringent the scene played, the more extensive the aftercare should be. Remember that you're essentially the owner of your sub and although you can do what you want with her during a scene, you're also bound to take care of her afterwards.

Chapter 5: Outside the Dungeon: Getting Started

Now that you have a pretty good idea of how the Dom role works, the next step is to find the BDSM community that will help you expand your knowledge on the subject and indulge your kinky desires. Now, there are several ways to get started on this:

Finding a Partner

If you're lucky enough to have a partner who is also into BDSM, then there should be no need to seek out the BDSM community in your area. You and your partner may enjoy the relationship without question, allowing yourselves to play any scene you wish when it comes to BDSM.

Some Doms like to post advertisements through websites like Craigslist or perhaps internet communities specially set up for the BDSM scene. Although this is certainly a possibility, do not keep your hopes up that a sub will respond, especially if the setup is in your house. This is because as already mentioned, the Dom/sub relationship is anchored on trust. In a BDSM scene, the sub is highly vulnerable so there's very little chance the she will play with someone she only met through the internet.

BDSM Dungeons

The best way therefore to find a sub and to exercise your BDSM predilections is through Dungeons. Typically, Dungeons are paid-for facilities where you can hire either a Dom or a sub to play a scene with you. There are several advantages here including the fact that you'll be meeting with people who are in the same mindset as you. Additionally, dungeons are staffed by individuals who have a pretty good grip on the BDSM lifestyle and can provide you with the exact experience you want. In many cases, dungeons will guide you through the process, talk about how it works, and what can be expected.

The best thing about dungeons however, is that it helps you build a reputation. Once the community manages to see how well you take the role of a Dom, you'll be more welcomed into the lifestyle and subs will be more willing to play with you under different scenes. In some instances, you may find a sub to play with outside the dungeon.

Munch

Playing in dungeons or searching the internet can get you invited for your very first Munch. As already defined, a Munch is a gathering where BDSM enthusiasts meet in a public place for socialization purposes. This is a great way to be introduced to the society, allowing you to interact with people who follow the same lifestyle. Take advantage of your first Munch and ask different questions about BDSM and how you can proceed further into the lifestyle.

Dungeon versus Personal Play

The main difference between the two is that Dungeon Plays are often highly regulated. This means that actual sex or facsimiles thereof are often not allowed. Hence, penetration by the penis or any object in the vagina or anus is often disallowed. Instead, the pain and discomfort themselves are the replacement for the erotic component of the sex. Of course, this is not a general rule. Depending on your dungeon, the sex may or may not be allowed. Note though that generally speaking, sex combined with BDSM in an official dungeon would be termed prostitution, and therefore illegal.

Personal Plays however, typically have the element of sex into them. The sub and Dom may play with the intent of achieving orgasm at some point. Since there's usually a personal relationship during such plays, there is no problem as to the legal aspect of the whole thing.

National Kink Coming Out Day

If you feel like you're ready to show the world how kinky you are, then you can also participate in the National Kink Coming Out Day. This is a special event wherein individuals who happen to love BDSM and revel in the lifestyle come out and socialize with like minded individuals. You might want to check out this particular event and find out how you can get started as a member of the BDSM community.

BDSM Etiquette

Do NOT use the toys of other Doms for their subs. In fact, etiquette requires that you should NOT touch the toy of other Doms unless specifically allowed. The same holds true for your toys. Also note that having your own toys, whether you play in a dungeon or not is important, especially if you play with only one sub. This is for the interest of safety and health security as bodily fluids can often come up during a scene. Washing your toys should be done after every scene.

Chapter 6: More BDSM Techniques for the Bolder Dom

Being the Dominant requires that you know a lot of techniques. Otherwise, the submissive will not writhe in fear, pain, and pleasure altogether. These elements are important in BDSM, especially if you want to play the really aggressive Dom. Here are more techniques to make your play more exciting and heart-pounding:

1. USING SEX TOYS

   - You could insert connected beads to your vagina or anus then have them pulled out.

   - Use dildos (a non-vibrating phallus) to add stimulation.

   - You could use love eggs, otherwise known as oriental eggs. These are two balls connected that you place inside the body. It is powered by battery.

   - Play with suction toys on your breasts, nipples, or genitals.

   - As a Dom, use vibrator on your sub for internal and external stimulation.

2. THROUGH BONDAGE

   - Bondage Light. You could lightly bind the body to make the sub feel he/she is really a slave.

   - Bondage Heavy, where the sub is not allowed any movement.

- Place your sub in a box or a closet.

- Bind his/her breasts.

- Put your sub in a cage and play pretend that he/she be freed if he/she does as you say.

- Affix your sub on a post, as if you're crucifying the sub.

- Bind the sub's whole body.

- Bind the sub's genitals.

- Hypnotize your sub and make him/her submit freely to you.

- Wrap your sub in leather, cotton, or whatever tickles your fantasy.

- Restrain your sub outdoors or privately.

- Show other people that you are restraining your sub. The restraint could take an hour or more, even overnight. You could even restrain your sub for days, unless the sub says a safeword.

- Suspend your sub above the ground, whether vertically or horizontally. The sub can also be suspended upside down.

3. USING BONDAGE TOYS

- Blindfolds are effective in heightening other senses in a sub other than sight.

- Place the sub in a body bag, or restrict his/her movement with a duct tape.

- Make the sub wear hoods to allow a small part of the fabric for breathing or seeing.

- Gag your partner with a ball, cloth, a bit, a dildo, or any inflatable device. Duct tapes can also be used to gag the sub.

- Use a harness for your sub. Choose from leather or rope.

- Deprive your sub of hearing by making him/her wear earplugs.

- Use a metal bondage equipment such as manacles.

- Cover your or your sub's face with a mask. It adds excitement.

- Use bondage that can be freed by a key.

- Bind the sub's ankles and arms. Use handcuffs as restraint.

- In place of leather and rope, use silk scarves to restrict the sub's body.

- Place the sub in a sleep sack to immobilize him/her.

- Put the sub in a swing or a sling. Restrict the sub's movement by connecting his/her legs to a spreader bar. Strait jackets are also quite popular nowadays.

4. THROUGH SADOMASOCHISM

- Scrape or scratch the skin of your partner. You could use your nails or any abrasive material.

- Stretch the sub's anus open. This is called anal dilation. You could also place your hand inside the sub's anus.

- Asphyxiate the sub by covering his/her face with a cloth or a thin plastic.

- Torture the sub's soles (bastinado). Beat your partner lightly or heavily. Use your arms or a paddle. You could beat any part of the body for that matter (e.g. the back, the butt, chest, breast, feet, genitals, or the face). The severity of beating depends on the slave contract, however. Make sure that you inflict the right amount of pain. The logic of BDSM is to give pain as much as pleasure.

- Bite your partner. Nibble on the skin until there are red marks. This is also a method of branding, though the marks will not be permanent.

- Stretch or milk the breast. You could also do breast torture or breast whipping.

- Choke your partner, but not to the extent that he/she loses oxygen entirely.

- Use electricity to create pain or sensation.

- Slap the submissive's face. This is better done when the sub is feeling so much pleasure already.

- Use fire and heat to increase sexual sensations.

- Pull the hair of your sub. Pinch the skin, or punch a body part.

- Give your partner a scar that he/she will always remember you by. The more personal the scar, the better it is.

- Scratch the skin of your partner especially when both of you are enjoying the sexual act. Spank the sub, whether the sub is on hands and knee. Spanking can be hard or soft.

- Deliberately stretch the vagina of your submissive, or do vaginal fisting (place your hand inside her).

- If the sub is female, make her wear a bodice or a corset and tighten it. While in the act, her breasts will bulge and there will be pain. Say that you'll release the hold on the bodice if the sub is willing to be "a good girl".

There are other methods, but these are already within vanilla sex, and may not be considered BDSM techniques. A word of caution: Always make sure that your partner consents to the act. You don't want to be labeled "unsafe".

BDSM is all about entertainment. Whether you want to inflict pain or not, the bottom line is that both you and your partner should benefit from the sexual activity. After all, BDSM was meant for play, not for abuse. Whatever happens in the dungeon should stimulate you and your sub. A real Dom is in control of the play, while beginners simply experiment without any thoughts of aftercare.

BDSM is also not just about physical play. There is also mental play here. The most important thing as the Dom is that you and your sub know who's in charge in the dungeon. The switch will be good for both sexes, and there would be no struggle for power. There is only surrender.

Chapter 7: Qualities of a Dominant

In order to be a dominant , you are going to make sure that you exhibit some very important qualities that are going to determine if you are successful or not when it comes to being dominant . If you cannot show all of these qualities, you may end up being a dominant that does not have a submissive, or you are going to become a dominant that is in a relationship that many people are not going to want to be with.

Self-control

If you are not able to control yourself such as your emotions, then you are not going to be able to control that in another person. Other dominant s are going to see you as weak and too self-indulgent therefore you are not going to have the skills necessary to control how someone else is going to react emotionally. It does not matter how good your submissive is, there are going to be times that they are going to act out and resist your control. However, how you deal with that resistance is going to be what is going to encourage your submissive to give you good behavior or is going to encourage that bad behavior. The better that you can deal with their emotional outbursts, the better they are going to be as well as the happier they are because you are able to read their emotions and know what is going on and how to react to it before it gets out of hand.

A lot of the time, the problem that brings out anger or any other negative emotion is going to be that your submissive has a problem submitting and you are going to have to work that out of them. Having self-control means that you are going to be able to react to the outbursts of your submissive in a controlled manner instead of overreacting and possibly damaging your relationship with your submissive. Together you can work on a plan that is going to discourage negative behavior.

Stubbornness and emotional resilience

When you are a dominant , you are going to have to be able to create a relationship with your submissive that is going to make it to where you get what you want without having to push your submissive to a point where you damage your relationship with them. Being stubborn can be a good trait, however you do not want to push it too far or else you are going end up coming off like a child who is throwing a fit that they did not get their way. Remember that any resistance that you are met with is going to be because the submissive is having a problem with submitting. Just like was discussed in the self-control section, you are going to want to be able to control your emotions so that you are not having an outburst each time that your submissive does something that you do not like. Instead, relish in the resistance that you come up against and let it enhance your control over your submissive.

Responsibility

As a dominant you are responsible for not only yourself, but for someone else. You have to be able to have enough responsibility to know that when you are participating in play, you are not only thinking about yourself. It is in these times that your submissive is going to get harmed. You need to make sure that you are putting your submissive first because in the end, it is the submissive that has the true power to say when everything is going to stop.

Whenever you speak and come to realize that you are angry, you need to be sure that you are thinking before you speak. What you do is going to affect your submissive as well as yourself. There are

46

going to be things that you are going to encounter that are only going to come from you because you are going to be the one who is in control of the boat that you are riding on. You have to realize that you are the one who is calling the shots and no one else.

Maturity

Once again, you are in charge of another human being. What happens to them is going to be based solely on what you decide to do. So, when something goes wrong, you cannot blame what happened on someone else. You have to step up and take responsibility for the things that you do wrong and make it right. Having power over someone else is going to make it difficult to achieve your goals and it is going to take a while for you to actual achieve the relationship that you are wanting to have with your submissive.

Being mature means that you are going to be able to be an example that your submissive can look up to and be proud of. In a dominant the submissive is going to find strength and support all of the time not just when it is convenient for him. Also, being mature means that you are going to recognize that life happens and that he cannot control everything.

You should never learn this by experimenting on your submissive! This should be something that you learn elsewhere where you are not having complete control over someone's life.

Trustworthiness

Your submissive needs to be able to put their complete trust in you. You are going to doing things to your submissive that they are not going to allow another living soul to do and if they cannot trust you completely, then how are they going to trust that you are not going to harm them?

Not only does your submissive need to be able to trust you with their body, but they also need to be able to trust you with their emotions as well. They have to know that they are going to be able to come to you with any problem that they may have and you are not going to push them away or reject them in anyway.

What does not seem like a big deal to you may be earth shattering for someone else. So, when your submissive comes to you with a problem, they have to know that you are not only going to keep it to yourself, but you are going to do everything in your power to fix it for them.

Experience and knowledge

You need to know what you are doing! There are some dominant s out there that start out as a dominant because they want to know what they are putting someone else through. While this is not going to be a requirement, it is a good place to start for some because they do not know exactly what it is that they are getting into.

You should never stop learning either. You need to keep up to date on all the information that you can possibly find so that you are not doing something that is frowned upon in the BDSM community if you participate in it.

Besides, it is a good idea to have some firm data to fall back on when you are doubting yourself. And, do not overthink things. It takes a long time to be able to know how to control someone and how that type of relationship is going to work.

Do not be afraid to ask for a mentor in the BDSM community. Having someone who is out there for you to pick their brain or ask questions when things start going south is helpful and will assist you when it comes to making sure that you are doing things the right way.

Desire

The sad thing about some people is that they are fine with someone else for short periods of time, but when it comes to being around someone all the time, they have no idea what to do to keep the relationship going.

Being a dominant is not always about controlling the other person and having sex with them all the time. You have to actually get to know the other person. You are spending considerable amounts of time with this person and you are going to want to know all that you can about them.

The more that you know, the easier it is going to be to understand what they are going through and you are also going to know when something is wrong even when they do not say anything.

Chapter 8: Rules for a Dom

When you are a dominant , there are things that you are going to want to keep in mind as you go about your life. Being a dominant is not something that you can just turn off and turn back on when the situation is right. It is something that you are going to have to experience every day of your life. You have to think of your submissive in everything that you do because whether you know it or not, what you decide to do is going to affect them in one way or another.

1. Safety has to be your top priority. This does not just mean that you have to worry about their physical safety but their emotional safety as well. It does not mean that you are the one who is harming them. Sometimes they harm themselves and you have to protect them from themselves as well as other people. If you see that there is something that is harming them, you need to make sure that you are protecting them so that it does not continue to happen.

2. Communication. Sometimes people forget that communicating is key. But, in a BDSM relationship, you have to be able to communicate. The submissive needs to feel like they are able to come to you about their needs, what they want to try, and even what they may be concerned about. The same should go for you. You do not need to be giving yourself up just to make your submissive happy. Dominant , submissive relationships are a give and take on both ends.

3. Trust your submissive or else your submissive is going to start to push you away. Why should they keep trying if all they feel they are doing is failing you? You should be able to trust your

partner until they show you that you cannot. And that goes the other way as well. Your partner needs to

be able trust you completely.

4. Whenever punishment is being administered when you are angry. If you are angry when punishment comes to from you, it should be in a loving manner and not because you cannot control your anger. If you are not able to control your anger, that is when you need to walk away and deal with it later. Be sure that you explain why you acted the way that you did. And, if you do end up finding that you punish when you are angry, you stand up and claim what you did and apologize. Then you need to make it right so that your submissive does not think that this is going to happen all of the time. Also, you should explain what it is that you are expecting out of your submissive in the future when it comes to that situation.

5. Do not be afraid to admit that you have made a mistake. You are human. However, you do not need to keep going without acknowledging that you have made a mistake or that you are blaming it on someone else. your relationship is going to continue to grow by admitting that you have made a mistake.

6. Encourage your submissive. Help her grow and do not tell her that she cannot do what she wants to do. If she has dreams, push her towards them. Your goal is to make sure that she is not staying still in life because she is not allowing you to stay static so, why should she? The more that you grow together, the better your relationship is going to be.

7. You do not know it all! Never assume that you know everything because there are always things that you are going to be able to

learn. Pick up books and read them to stay up to date on the most recent information. Read articles, and as we said earlier, do not be afraid to get a mentor.

8. Make sure that your submissive has no questions about your boundaries. You cannot just go make new rules whenever you feel like you should punish your submissive. Make sure that they know where the lines are and that if they cross them, then they are going to be punished for doing something that they know not to do.

9. Be sure to tell your submissive that you value her. You may not love your submissive like a husband loves a wife, and no one is expecting that of you. However, your submissive is doing something for you and giving up a big part of their life, so value your submissive and do not only tell her, but show her!

10. Never abandon your submissive. If there comes a time that you think that your relationship with your submissive has to end, be sure that you talk to them about it. Up until the relationship is terminated, you are responsible for your submissives emotional state.

Chapter 9: Signs of Someone Who is a Non-Dominant

There are some people that are going to act as if they are dominant s and they tend to get people hurt because they are doing something that they have no need to be doing because they do not have the proper knowledge that is going to ensure that they are not going to harm someone.

Sometimes it is hard to tell a true dominant from someone who is just playing. Even as another dominant , you need to be able to find those that are imposters because they can end up harming someone and you are going to feel like it is your fault that you did not do something when you could have.

1. While control is part of a dominant and submissive relationship, the control that a non-dominant exhibits is not going to be because it is part of the relationship. Instead, it is because they feel like they are going to lose their partner and if they are not controlling, they are going to walk out and be alone. There are a few things that they do in order to control their partner to ensure that they are not going to be able to go anywhere.

   a. They show jealousy that is well beyond what it needs to be. A little jealousy is normal, but there is a line and someone who is not a true dominant is going to cross this line.

   b. The submissive is going to be isolated from their friends and family. This is going to take a little bit of time doing but eventually they are not going to talk to any of their family or friends because they are going to feel like they will be punished if they do. This is one way that the non-dominant makes sure that the submissive cannot leave because they have nowhere to go.

   c. Social interactions do not happen without the dominant being there. This is because the dominant thinks that a simple interaction such as ordering food at a restaurant is going to come off as flirting and thus will start a relationship with that person which gives the submissive somewhere to go.

   d. When a submissive shows that they are able to do something for themselves, someone who is not a dominant is going to discourage that because once the submissive is able to do something that not only pushes themselves forward, but could end up getting them out of the relationship, the dominant is going to be left alone.

2. Their temper is explosive. The littlest thing will set a non-dominant off. This can be as simple as the wrong word being spoken or something major like a decision being made that should have been a group decision.

3. Whenever a non-dominant does not get their way, they are going to throw a temper tantrum. This is because they believe that they are supposed to always get their way because they are the ones that are in control and no one else should be able to get what they want until the non-dominant gets what they want.

4. Drugs and alcohol are usually abused and this can lead to some of the explosive behavior that is seen.

5. Whenever mistakes are made, the non-dominant is going to not take responsibility for their own actions. Instead, he is going to blame whoever is most convenient at the time.

6. Other unhealthy behavior choices are going to be made in order to make sure that the submissive is going to be kept under his thumb. This can be any number of things that can be considered abuse in a relationship.

   a. Withdrawal of affection or emotional withdrawal. In order to get their way, they are going to do the silent treatment or refuse to give their submissive intimacy so that the submissive is fearful that the relationship is going to end.

   b. Emotional blackmail. When the submissive is scared that if they do not give into what the non-dominant wants, then they are going to do whatever it is that the non-dominant wants. This is also a way for the submissive to try and make sure that the black mail that the non-dominant is holding does not get out to anyone else.

A non-dominant is going to be really good at making others believe that he is a true dominant, but you have to keep an eye on the warning signs. The first person who is going to be able to tell you about the warning signs is the submissive. However, you do not need to overstep your bounds being that it is not your submissive as well as the fact that they may be scared to speak up and save themselves.

Conclusion

Thank you again for downloading this book!

Other than the rules when it comes to safety, there are no defined limits as to the practice of BDSM. The only requirements are that they are sane, safe, and consensual as originally talked about in the previous Chapter. As a Dom, here's what you should keep in mind before, during, and after a play:

- Always ask the sub what they're willing and not willing to do

- Always ask for consent

- Always exercise self control

- Always practice aftercare

BDSM is a unique community filled with people from all sides of the community. You might be surprised, but the truth is that some members come from the higher ranks of society who simply have very different preferences in their lifestyle. As long as it does not cause harm to anyone else, BDSM is a perfectly acceptable way of life.

The next step is to apply these tips and strategies to bring your sex life and your relationship to exhilarating heights.

Lastly, remember that sex is meant to be an extraordinary experience, so don't be afraid of exploring activities and sensations that are beyond the ordinary. Each of us has our own fetishes and fantasies. Are you brave enough to live out yours?

Finally, if you enjoyed this book, then I'd like to ask you for a favor; would you be kind enough to leave a review for this book on Amazon? It'd be greatly appreciated!

Thank you and good luck!

BONUS: Preview of our fiction book Taming the Tigress: A Journey To Submission

Chapter 1: Caged

Punishment

I awoke in pitch blackness. I was all alone. I waited for it to come... the dread, the panic. It didn't. At first, I thought that the cold had numbed me, body and soul. But then I remembered. And I felt the stirrings of excitement in my gut, the involuntary clench of my cunt, triggered by the remembrance of the night before.

Was it really last night that he came here? Or was it the night before that? I could scarcely remember.

In the dungeon, there were neither days nor nights. Only darkness bleeding into further darkness. I counted my days not by the mornings or the evenings. No, the Master was my universe, my rising and my setting sun. My days began with his touch. And my days died each time he left. His touch... oh I tried to remember it. I shivered in the cold and tried to recall the warmth of his hands encircling my ankles, travelling up my legs, my thighs, tracing the triangle of my pubic hair. He took his sweet time knowing fully well how he was torturing me. At this memory, lust spread like wildfire all over my body. I remembered everything with stunning precision although the occasions when he would actually touch me seemed so rare compared to the moments I spent alone in the dungeon.

I felt the ache in my stretched muscles. In the dungeon, every single inch of my body was alive with pain. Yet every fiber of my being tingled with excitement. My hands were cuffed and tied to a high pole. My legs were spread wide apart. My toes were barely touching the cold stone floor. Time trundled at a snail's pace and I spent the hours wavering between consciousness and unconsciousness, teetering between sanity and madness. I would strain my ears listening to the sounds of his footsteps, hoping he would come. There were times when I could've sworn I heard his footsteps. They were heavy, leisurely, torturous... Yet I would hear the sound stop just outside the door. I would hear the rasping sound of his breathing, sense the heat of his body from the other side. At those times, I would be tempted to call out his name, to beg him to come to me. But then I'd remember what the Master had said to me: "Not a sound, *mon chaton*."

Ah yes, he called me his kitten. I was his pet. His strokes were always gentle. Until I misbehaved. Then he brought me to the dungeon.

Once, I dared myself to call him. Just once. Just so I could feel him near me again. When I first opened my mouth, it was as if my tongue had been severed. I tried to scream out his name but it came out as a dry croak. My throat was parched. I hadn't drunk anything in days.

He saw me, of course. I had no idea how many hours he spent looking at me from the monitor in his bedroom.

He came for me then. My Master, my Savior. A weak yellow light tiptoed into the room and I felt the familiar damp sensation spreading between my thighs. The Master carried a gas lamp in one hand and a bucket of water in the other.

He let me drink tiny sips from his open palms. I licked his palms clean, wasting not a single drop. I kept licking his palms, flicking my tongue against his hard flesh. He flipped his hand and I licked the back of it, lovingly, eagerly; perhaps a bit too eagerly because he pulled it suddenly away from me.

I looked into his eyes beseechingly. *Please, take me.* I thought, though I dared not speak the words out loud. *Please.*

He shook his head slowly. Then he walked away, leaving me sobbing in the dark. I knew then that that was my punishment for attempting to speak.

Reward

I knew that my obedience would not be for nothing. I heard his footsteps. They were quick, decisive, urgent.

The Master wanted me and he wanted me then and there.

The door swung open and I kept my gaze downward, not daring to ruin things by being too presumptuous. His breathing was heavy and I saw the bulk of his cock straining rebelliously against the fabric of his trousers. I knew my obedience had turned him on. Inside, I rejoiced. I knew I did well. I behaved and stayed put and waited for him in that dungeon. It was time for my reward.

He produced the key from his pocket and yet despite his obvious urgency, he unlocked the cuffs and untied the ropes slowly. My knees were so weak and my muscles were extremely exhausted that I fell towards him.

The Master caught me in his arms. His breath was hot in my ear as he whispered: "Lie down, Katharine."

I lay down and the coldness of the stone was cruel. It didn't matter.

"Good, my pet." he said. "Now, keep your hands on your sides."

So I did. My legs were splayed, ready to receive him. My palms flat on the floor.

The Master knelt in front of me, unzipped his trousers and freed his furious flesh.

He grabbed my ankles and raised my legs so they were pointing toward the ceiling. Then he pushed them down towards me so that my feet were on either side of my head. I became extremely aware of how exposed I was to him.

Without warning, he impaled me with a single penetrating fuck. He pierced me, flesh and soul. I screamed with pleasure and gratitude.

He moved in and out of me and with each filling thrust, his balls slapped hard against my cunt. My moist cunt involuntarily convulsed around his rigid cock and my love liquid poured generously around him.

He gasped.

I looked up to see his handsome leonine face. It was contorted in ecstasy. For a brief moment, just before he shuddered and released his hot spunk into me, I caught a glimpse of a side of him that I rarely saw.

I always wished I could freeze time, capture that image of him, and hold it forever. But right now, I am his slave. He is my Master.

How did I get here?

I *wanted* to be here, had begged to be here. I wanted to surrender my life into his hands.

Chapter 2: The Tigress

How did I get here?

It all started with an awkward incident at the ladies' room.

"The Tigress was at it again this morning." said the whiny voice that trickled from the bathroom stall. "I find it really hard to concentrate on my work when she's like literally breathing down my neck."

Laughter oozed from the other stall. "Looks like someone needs to get laid."

My first reaction was fury. Who the fuck do these bitches think they are? They work for *me*. Then I realized how pathetic that sounded. Me, bullied by my own employees. I didn't even know what their names were or what departments they're from.

The Tigress. That's what they called me. I used to think that it was a fond nickname, owing to my fierceness and my success. Until I realized that it wasn't.

I waited for the women to come out. When they did, I looked at their pale faces and said: "You're fired. Both of you."

Then I left, feeling terrible over my extreme immaturity.

"They *love* working for you." Joan, my secretary, who is also coincidentally my only friend at the office, told me. "But they also hate working for you. If that makes any sense…"

It did make sense. I was too uptight. My ill temper was contagious. Somehow, with my controlling attitude, I created a hostile work environment for my employees.

I decided to take the afternoon off and asked Joan to cancel my next two appointments.

"How did the delivery go?" I picked up my purse, ready to leave.

I was talking about the anonymous client who ordered chartreuse silk dresses by the bulk. Here's the catch: Through the past year, it was always several pieces of the exact same design, color, and size. It was weird. The money, though, was always paid up front. In fact, I owed the expansion of my little dress shop partly to that client's patronage. So I figured, if she wanted to use that single design as some sort of disposable daily uniform, then so be it.

That's not to say that I hadn't been curious. In fact, I used to be the one who personally delivered the dresses to the mansion. It was always received by different maids whose bland faces betrayed nothing. I knew that the mansion was owned by Louis Archambault as in Archambault Pharmaceuticals. But as far as I knew, there was no Mrs. Archambault.

I tried Googling him, of course. Apparently, he's a very private person. He was handsome, disturbingly so; a tall man with piercing eyes. In his photos, his lips were curled to form a curt half-smile... a cold, almost cruel curve. But I had a feeling that they could be warm and tender when he wanted them to be.
I even went so far as to send him a thank you gift: a dress of a different design. Then I got flowers and a formal thank you note, no doubt written by his secretary. After a while, I just gave up trying to find out who the gowns were for. For all I knew, they were

64

for him. Still, for some ridiculous reason, I kept his picture in one of my folders. I looked at it from time to time.

"They're still here." Joan's voice punctured my thoughts.

"What?"

"The gowns are still here. Winona was supposed to deliver them."

"Well, why didn't she?" I asked, starting to get irritated.

"Um, you just fired her..."

"Shit."

#

Before I could even bother to introduce myself, the new maid ushered me into the house while the other unloaded the boxes from my car. It was my first time to see the mansion's interior. It was palatial.

"You're late." she scolded.

"Oh." I said. "I know. I'm so--"

"Shush!" She cut me off, harshly. "He'll be here soon. Let's get you ready."

I hardly paid attention to what she said after that. I let her drag me up the stairs.

He'll be here soon... That was all I could think about. *Him!*

So I played along, not thinking about the consequences.

Until then, it didn't really occur to me how badly I wanted to meet him. One peek, I told myself. And then I'll come clean.

When she slipped me into one of the silk dresses, I realized that it was my size.

So, I thought. *Mr. Archambault likes his escorts in my green dresses.* And the maid mistook me for one of them. I wasn't exactly sure how I felt about that.

I was led into his office.

And there he was in all his dominant glory.

"Sit." he said sharply.

I found myself automatically dropping into a chair.

"Not there." He said again. He pressed his hand on his desk. "Here."

There was a magnetism in his voice that I couldn't resist. Without peeling my gaze from his lion-like face and without understanding myself, I sat on the edge of the table.

When his fingers dug into my shoulders, I felt the energy from his touch. The current traveled all the way from my shoulders to my clit. I pressed my legs together. I was starting to get wet.
He lifted my skirt and pried my legs open with one swift gesture. Blood rushed to my face as I realized that he was smiling at the swiftly spreading puddle of pussy juice on my panties.

I opened my mouth but my indignant protest came out as a gasp.

He had entered me with his fingers, a heavenly assault.

Then, he withdrew his hand up to his lips to taste me.

"It's nice to finally meet you, Ms. Mallory."

He flashed me his cold, cruel half-grin and for a fleeting moment, I felt fear.

Instinctively, I got to my feet and raised my hand to slap him. But he caught it and in one deft movement, he turned me over so that I was leaning facedown onto the table.

He pulled down my panties. I felt his erection pressing against my ass. I trembled with anticipation. I expected him to enter me roughly from behind.

Slap!

The ruler landed on my bum, causing the flesh to sting.

Then he ran his palm soothingly over my smarting butt cheeks.

"I do not tolerate tardiness." he said.

Slap!

The ruler came down, harder this time.

Was he *punishing* me?

I ought to have stopped him. I ought to have run away. I ought to have done a lot of things.

But I stayed.

Slap!

Tears stung my eyes.

"*Never* raise your hand against me!" he said roughly into my ear.

I heard the silk ripping away beneath his hands. My body flooded with proportionate amounts of lust and fear.

"Beautiful." he sighed. "You are a blank canvass."

But he didn't fuck me like I hoped he would.

Instead, I listened to his breath waxing and waning as he masturbated.

I tried to face him but he held my head down, my cheeks pressed hard against the table.

"Stay down." he ordered. "You are no lioness. You are my little kitten. That's all you are, *mon chaton.*"

"Yes." I murmured, tears stinging my eyes. "Yes."

I felt him shudder. And a deluge of hot semen rained down my back and trickled down my still burning bum.

He walked away, leaving me there, bent over, covered in his jizz, my cunt still wet and aching for him.

I cried. At that moment, I knew. He broke me. And I've never felt more alive.

CPSIA information can be obtained
at www.ICGtesting.com
Printed in the USA
BVHW040148120620
581323BV00009B/501

9 789198 604788